Your Guide to the Stars of "Beverly Hills, 90210"

One is a farmer's daughter from Illinois. Another was discovered in a grocery store. And another had been acting since the age of four. Do you know who's who on "Beverly Hills, 90210"?

- Who just received his bachelor's degree?

- Which star credits his dyslexia for pushing him into acting?

- Which real-life twin won a scholarship to study with the San Francisco Ballet, then traveled all over Europe performing as a mime artist?

- Which star is *least* like the character he plays?

- How did they break into show business?

Everything you want to know is here in the book that goes behind the scenes of the show that's making TV history!

Books by Daniel Cohen

BEVERLY HILLS, 90210: Meet the Stars of Today's Hottest
 TV Series
GOING FOR THE GOLD: Medal Hopefuls for Winter '92
 (with Susan Cohen)
THE GREATEST MONSTERS IN THE WORLD
THE MONSTERS OF STAR TREK
MONSTERS YOU NEVER HEARD OF
REAL GHOSTS
THE RESTLESS DEAD: Ghostly Tales from Around the World
STRANGE AND AMAZING FACTS ABOUT STAR TREK

Available from ARCHWAY Paperbacks

GHOSTLY TERRORS
PHONE CALL FROM A GHOST: Strange Tales from Modern
 America
THE WORLD'S MOST FAMOUS GHOSTS

Available from MINSTREL BOOKS

Beverly Hills, 90210

AN UNAUTHORIZED BIOGRAPHY

MEET THE STARS
of Today's Hottest TV Series

DANIEL COHEN

AN ARCHWAY PAPERBACK
Published by POCKET BOOKS
New York   London   Toronto   Sydney   Tokyo   Singapore

AN ARCHWAY PAPERBACK *Original*

An Archway Paperback published by
POCKET BOOKS, a division of Simon & Schuster Inc.
1230 Avenue of the Americas, New York, NY 10020

Copyright © 1991 by Daniel Cohen

ISBN: 0-671-77052-7

First Archway Paperback printing November 1991

10 9 8 7 6 5 4 3 2 1

AN ARCHWAY PAPERBACK and colophon are registered trademarks of Simon & Schuster Inc.

Printed in the U.S.A.

IL 5+

To IBM Wheelwriter 50 Series II

CONTENTS

Contents

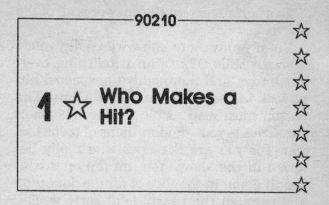

1 ☆ Who Makes a Hit?

Who made "Beverly Hills, 90210" the hottest TV show for teens in years, perhaps the hottest TV show for teens ever?

Is it the stars like Jason Priestley, Shannen Doherty, and Luke Perry?

Is it legendary TV producer Aaron Spelling?

Is it thirty-year-old creator-writer-supervising producer Darren Star?

Is it newly successful writer and executive producer Charles Rosin, or the husband-wife team of Steve Wasserman and Jessica Klein, the series story editors?

Is it the brash and innovative Fox TV network?

To a certain extent the answer is all of the above.

But if you want to know who really made "Beverly Hills, 90210" an astonishing, overwhelming, and thoroughly unexpected hit, go look in the mirror and take a bow. The person most responsible for the success of the series is you—and millions of teens like you. For you are the ones who really believed in the show. You are the ones who kept it going in the face of all the doubters, and through the nearly fatal early weeks. You are the ones who grabbed the TV moguls by the lapels and shouted, "Hey, this show is great! I know Brandon and Brenda and Dylan! I know what they are going through! And I want to see more of them!"

Every year there are *hundreds* of ideas for TV series. The ideas are discussed in heated meetings in producers' offices. They are discussed over expensive lunches in trendy Los Angeles and New York restaurants. They are discussed by phone, by letter, and by fax. Every idea sounds great—at first. But most of these ideas go absolutely nowhere. They just disappear during the first or second meeting.

There are a million reasons for killing an idea: It's been done before and the public is tired of it. It's never been done before, so how do we know if it will work? The advertisers won't like it. It's too daring for TV. It's not daring enough for today's TV. It's too expensive. No one is doing that kind of show this year. I like the idea, but I don't think we can sell it to the executives. I like the idea, but we'll never be able to sell it to the public. I don't like the idea. It might go in New York, but it will bomb in Kansas. It might go in Kansas, but it will bomb in New York. We'll never be able to get her to do a series. Who ever heard of that guy? You can't do a show with people no one ever heard of. Sure everybody knows him, but look what happened to his last show. And on and on.

Miraculously some of the ideas actually make it beyond the talking stage. Scripts are written and passed around. Market studies are done. Experts are consulted. Some of the scripts are optioned. Money changes hands. But most of the scripts wind up in some forgotten file. It is as if they never existed.

A few of the hardy ideas survive to the point where a pilot, or sample show, is made. But even at this point the attrition rate is extremely high. Most of the pilots that are shopped around are never purchased. Outside of the TV industry and possibly a few select test audiences, no one ever sees the pilots. Occasionally they will show up during the summer rerun season as "specials."

The process isn't very efficient. A tremendous amount of time, money, and talent is wasted on projects that go absolutely nowhere. Some worthwhile ideas die on the vine. But to be absolutely honest, most of the projects deserve to die. If you make it a habit of watching those orphan pilots during the summer you may wonder how such a stupid idea for a show got as far as it did. In fact, you may ask the same question when viewing some of the shows that actually do make it into the regular season lineup. What were all those high-priced and supposedly creative people thinking when they put this mess together?

It costs megamillions to launch a new TV series, even a low-budget TV series. Before that kind of money is spent, the producers and the studios want to be as sure as they possibly can that the series will be a hit or, at the very least, that it will survive long enough to make some money.

The amount of money that can be made by all connected with a major TV series is absolutely mind-boggling. But then, the amount of money that can be made by winning the lottery is also mind-boggling. And there are more similarities between winning the lottery and putting together a hit TV series than most of the experts would like to admit.

After the show climbs up in the ratings, all the TV experts can dissect the elements and explain why it worked. But the very same experts are not nearly as clever at predicting which shows will be a hit before they are aired for the public. The fact is that no matter how many experts are consulted, no matter how many polls are taken and audience studies made, no one really knows which shows will work and which will die. Most shows either die or struggle on gamely for a season or two before passing into total oblivion. When was the last time you heard of "Hull High"? Or what about . . . but no, I've already forgotten the title, and so has everyone else.

Want to have a little fun? Save the fall preview issue of *TV Guide* or your local newspaper's TV magazine. See what shows they predict will be successful. Then read the same articles over when the season ends and see how many of those predicted successes will be back next year. How many shows even survived the first season? It's a lot of laughs. It's almost as much fun as saving the New Year's predictions issues of supermarket tabloids to see how many of the psychics' predictions come true. The psychics are darn near as accurate as the

TV experts. Perhaps in their spare time they double as TV critics.

A lot of shows that have died a quick and ignominious death were highly touted and elaborately promoted. Other shows that were supposed to bomb are still around. The classic example is "Star Trek." A quarter-century after it first appeared, reruns, films, and videotapes are still popular. So is an extremely powerful sequel. "Star Trek" is more than a show; it's a cultural phenomenon and, for many, a way of life. Love it or hate it, you've heard of it. You can't escape it. It's always on television somewhere, sometime. But the highly paid network executives, who are supposed to know about such things, killed that show after a mere three seasons. They didn't think it could keep an audience. Do you remember the show that replaced it? No, neither do I.

What's the secret of a successful show? I don't know. If I did, I'd be the richest and most powerful man in show business. The point is that nobody else knows the secret, either. Oh, they can make educated guesses, but in the end it's like the lottery—a gamble. But the TV gamble doesn't cost just a buck or two to play. Producers, networks, and sponsors bet millions that they know what you are going to want to watch when you turn on the TV. You and people who are supposed to be just like you are constantly polled and questioned and prodded and probed by computer in order to find out, or to try to find out, what show you will tune in to when you turn on that set.

Heavy promotion can jump-start a show. Big-name stars can compel viewers to watch once or twice. Research can give producers, directors, and writers a general idea of what people want to watch. But in the end it is an almost magical bond between the audience and the show that elevates a series from just another TV offering to a hit, the kind of show that everyone is talking about, the show that you just can't afford to miss. And no one has been able to successfully explain how or why that magic works. Has anyone been able to figure out a formula for predicting the sort of person you are going to fall in love with? Of course not. You don't know, so how is anyone else supposed to know before it happens? Hit shows are like a love affair between the audience and the show, and there is no formula for predicting that, either.

And all of this brings us back to "Beverly Hills, 90210." This was a series that was never supposed to succeed. By all the rules of the TV business, it never should have been made in the first place. And once it was made, by all rights it should have disappeared into the great black hole that swallows up so many TV programs. And that's what very nearly happened.

But then you and millions like you said, "No! This show can't disappear. I *love* it!" And, well, the rest is TV history.

☆
☆
☆

2 ☆ A Shaky Start

☆
☆
☆
☆

The original inspiration for "Beverly Hills, 90210" came from Darren Star, a newcomer to the television wars. This was the first pilot he had ever written. The basic idea was simple enough. Take a couple of kids from the heartland of America—let's say cold and snowy Minnesota—and make those kids twins, a boy and a girl. Then plunk them down in southern California, amid the sun and surf. In fact, put them in the middle of rich and ritzy Beverly Hills, one of the wealthiest communities in America.

Surround these two kids and their sane, solid, and stable family with a bunch of friends from the Beverly Hills fast lane and see what happens. Life at West Beverly High may be more glamorous than life at your school. Your school probably doesn't have palm trees, either. The students drive more expensive cars and wear more expensive clothes. But it's still life. These teenagers have to deal with divorce, alcoholic parents, drunken driving, drugs, pregnancy, fear of AIDS, racial tensions and prejudice—the same problems faced by teens everywhere, even in high schools that don't have palm trees.

Make the show serious, but not heavy, not preachy. Throw in plenty of humor. Depend on tight scripts, good direction, and good acting rather than gimmicks. The show that Darren Star most frequently referred to was the critically acclaimed but now canceled "thirtysomething." He has light-heartedly referred to "90210" as "teensomething."

Star was able to interest the Fox network in his idea. Fox is the smallest and most adventuresome of the major TV networks. The network has scored big with such off-beat shows as "The Simpsons," "Married . . . With Children," and "In Living Color." The network has also tried hard to cultivate a young audience. Fox had previously had great success with the teen-oriented "21

Jump Street." It is a network willing to take chances because it has less to lose.

To put the show together Fox called legendary producer Aaron Spelling, who has his own production company. In the past Spelling has produced such megahits as "Dynasty," "The Love Boat," "The Mod Squad," and "Charlie's Angels." Spelling is not known for producing innovative shows, but he sure knows how to put together a popular show.

Still, Spelling had little experience in doing shows for teens. And when Fox called and asked him if he would like to do a high school show he wasn't exactly thrilled by the prospect. He recalls that his response was "Not particularly."

He said he didn't know how to do shows like "Ferris Bueller's Day Off" or "Parker Lewis Can't Lose." But after the idea was explained to him Spelling changed his mind. "I really got excited," he says now.

Among those gathered for the creative team were Steve Wasserman and Jessica Klein, the series' story editors, who had written for the popular and somewhat offbeat CBS show "Northern Exposure." Writer and executive producer Charles Rosin had produced several TV movies and was supervising producer of "Northern Exposure." Episode directors were drawn from among Hollywood's brighter young directing talent. They have included movie folk like Tim Hunter (*The River's Edge*) and Charles Braverman (*The Brotherhood of Justice*). All in all, this was a quality group, neatly balancing years of TV experience with youthful enthusiasm.

And then there was the cast. Well, we are going to have a lot more to say about the cast very shortly. Right now we're tracing the show's rocky early history. For the moment it's enough to say that the cast members were all professionals with solid backgrounds in TV acting. Some came from show-business families and had been before the cameras while they were infants. But they were not big-time stars. You might have seen them in other shows from time to time, but before "90210" you probably wouldn't have recognized or remembered their names.

Originally the show was called "Class of Beverly Hills," but somewhere along the line it was decided that the title was too pedestrian. The new plan was to keep the "Beverly Hills" and tack on the zip code of the glitzy area. The change turned out to be an inspired one, for today the show is invariably referred to simply as "90210."

It wasn't the only teen-oriented show to

be scheduled for the fall 1990 season. Fox already had "Parker Lewis Can't Lose," and NBC was debuting "Hull High" and "Ferris Bueller." These shows had received much more advance attention than "90210."

While the creative team around the series had great confidence in what they were doing, the Fox network apparently began to get cold feet. The network executives didn't seem to know what to do with this new show. They certainly had no idea what they had. It was slipped into the fall 1990 schedule with virtually no fanfare and no hype. If people wanted to see "Beverly Hills, 90210" they had to find out about it all by themselves. What's more, the show was scheduled on Thursday night opposite "Cheers," which for years has consistently been at or near the top of the Nielsen ratings. The Nielsen ratings, which are supposed to measure who is watching what and when, are sacred to the TV industry, even though their accuracy has been widely questioned. Most shows live or die by the ratings. Scheduling any show next to the powerhouse "Cheers" was a surefire formula for failure, and for most shows it would have resulted in a quick trip to the dustbin of TV history. But "90210" was lucky to be on a small network like Fox. The major networks— NBC, CBS, and ABC—have a stable full of backup shows to replace those that are languishing in the ratings, and both "Hull High" and "Ferris Bueller" were quickly canceled. Fox, however, had no such luxury. At first "90210" was a ratings disaster, but Fox had no replacement, particularly for a death spot like the one opposite "Cheers." So "90210" stayed in the lineup. But its future did not look bright. The odds against it being renewed in 1991 were very long indeed.

The TV critics weren't exactly enamored of the show, either. Howard Rosenberg of the *Los Angeles Times* dismissed it as just "a ZIP code for stereotypes and stock characters." Other critics, when they noticed the show at all, were no kinder. In a mock memo to high school faculty members, written in September 1991, after the show was an established success, Tom Gliatto and Michael Alexander of *People* magazine apologized for failing to anticipate what was going to happen: "To some extent, I take responsibility for having ignored '90210.' I made the mistake of reading newspaper critics instead of my daughter's diary."

Television viewers today may have as many as fifty channels to choose from at any given time. Yet with all of the shows competing for your attention, and without any help at all from the promotional wizards, you and millions like you began finding "90210." At first this audience attention was barely perceptible. There were letters from fans, including some deep and heartfelt letters, indicating how thoroughly and quickly many teens had identified with the kids at West Beverly High. Such letters make some impression on TV executives, but ratings weigh much more heavily.

"I *knew* the fans were there," creator Darren Star told *People*. "Teenagers really respond to what they like. And they like to see something that says 'I'm not alone.'"

There were more stirrings out there among the teen audience. Mail began pouring in by the sackload now. Ratings began to creep up slightly. There was no sudden upsurge, but it was encouraging. Most of all, when members of the show's staff got out among teenage viewers who had actually seen the show, they knew they had something. They knew they were reaching their audience. The kids were not only passively watching the show; they spent all of Friday morning discussing it. And they were telling their friends who had not yet been able to locate it amidst the fifty or so channels what they were missing and encouraged them to try harder next time. Many began taping the show so they could watch it again, and again. It had what is known in the industry as good word-of-mouth.

After the first few episodes, the quality of the show improved. The characters became more real, the stories were tougher and more pertinent, and the actors grew into their roles. Despite the slow and discouraging start, the "90210" team became more and more convinced that they had a winner, that they had created something really special. They worked harder.

By the third episode the members of the creative team were sure that if they just had a little more time the whole country would know what a good show it was. Now the trick was to make more viewers aware of "Beverly Hills, 90210" before it was allowed to die. At this point, says Rosin, they developed a strategy to promote the show. They made their move in December 1990.

"We were so marginal for so long," says Rosin, "we went in to the network and said, 'Listen, unless you start promoting us, no one's going to know we're here.'" This time Fox listened. Perhaps some of the executives had begun listening to their own children rather than just reading the numbers on the Nielsen charts.

As the new year began and the casts and crews of most low-rated shows began reading *Variety*, the "90210" team members were not on the lookout for new jobs, because the network had begun to give "90210" the attention it deserved. Ratings began to soar, and by February it had moved ahead of most of its competition and into the number two spot behind "Cheers" for its time slot. That was a remarkable rise for a previously unheralded show. Even the optimists had not predicted that. By the season's end in May, "90210" was nearing the top forty in the ratings. Not "Roseanne" yet, but not bad for a one-time basket case. The survival of the show into the next season was ensured. The TV world had begun to catch up with its audience.

"The core audience was always aware of it," said Rosin. "It's just in the calendar year '91 that the network really promoted the show."

Then Fox made a truly revolutionary programming move. As summer approaches and viewing traditionally drops off, most shows take a three-month vacation. During that time, reruns are aired. But Fox decided there would be no summer vacation for the kids at West Beverly High School. They prepared seven new episodes to be shown during the summer, in addition to the standard twenty-three episodes for the regular season. That made thirty shows, an unprecedented commitment to a new series.

"Thirty shows!" said Aaron Spelling. "It's a gamble, but I'll tell you, they've got guts." Of course Spelling was delighted: his production company stood to make a bundle. If the show bombed, Fox stood to lose millions, but the network was confident now.

The gamble paid off in a big way. The show gained viewers who had never seen "90210" but were tired of reruns and wanted to see something new. They liked what they saw and they stayed. By the end of the summer the show had rocketed into the top twenty on the Nielsens.

When the new semester began at West Beverly High School on September 12, 1991, no one in the television industry could say that "90210" was a neglected show anymore. Instead of sneering, the critics were searching around for deep psychological reasons for the show's success.

You don't have to search very far, says Darren Star. "Teenagers take themselves very seriously and really see their lives in terms of high dramatics, and I think the show represents that very well." In a swipe at other teen-oriented shows Star says, "Most shows for adolescents seem like they are written by fifty-year-olds who think teenagers behave like seven-year-olds." Adds writer Jessica Klein: "The show is very honest, and the characters don't always do the right thing, which is, I think, terrific."

One big reason for the show's tremendous popularity is that it does not condescend to its audience. It doesn't treat them like angels or idiots; it shows them as human beings.

3 ☆ Big Business

How big has "Beverly Hills, 90210" become? There are lots of ways to answer that question, but there is no doubt in anyone's mind that the series is big business, very big business indeed. Listen to Aaron Spelling, who has produced some of the hottest shows in TV history and who knows what big business is: "I thought 'The Mod Squad' and 'Charlie's Angels' got a lot of publicity in their heyday, but it doesn't compare to this. It's crazy. We have merchandising coming out of our ears. And now those actors can't even walk down the street."

A lot of the business success can be summed up in a word that people in TV use all the time—*demographics*. What matters is not just *how many* people are watching the show, but *who* is watching. Some shows, including "60 Minutes" and "Roseanne," usually rank higher in the all-powerful Nielsen ratings and will doubtless continue to do so. But sheer numbers of viewers are not everything. Those shows certainly do not rank higher among teenage viewers. Is capturing a teen audience profitable? Teens made New Kids on the Block America's richest entertainers this year. At last report "90210" was capturing a solid 58 percent of the teen audience—and that is absolutely incredible.

Let's put those numbers another way. In 287 out of every 1,000 homes with TV sets there are teens who watch "Beverly Hills, 90210." The nearest competitor in this age group is "The Simpsons," with 254. Do you remember how many rude Bart Simpson T-shirts, lunch boxes, school bags, and toys flooded the market a couple of years ago? That may be nothing compared to the "90210" items that are to come. But as befits the name Beverly Hills this show's merchandise will be more upscale.

There will be a whole line of "90210" clothes—T-shirts, jeans, shoes, and the like. As you should expect from a southern California show there will be beach towels, bathing suits, and other beachwear. There will of course be notebooks and other school supplies—the characters do go to West Beverly High *School*, after all, although few scenes are actually shot in the classroom, and homework . . . well, it doesn't interfere with life—for Dylan, at least.

Likenesses of Brandon, Brenda, Dylan, and the rest of the gang will be showing up on everything from greeting cards to bubble gum cards. And the actors themselves will be in great demand to appear in ads for any number of products. Plans to have them appear at in-store promotions will have to be handled with extreme care. In August 1991 Luke Perry showed up for a promotion at a south Florida shopping center and was greeted by a mob of ten thousand screaming fans. Publicity and promotion people love this sort of screaming-fan scenario, which makes a great spot on the local news shows, but this one was no stunt. It got completely out of hand.

"It's a little scary," says Luke. Completely out-of-control fans are always a worry for popular actors.

You have already seen the faces of Luke, Jason, Shannen, and many of the other "90210" regulars on the covers of all the teenage magazines. Expect to see them again and again. There are inserts and posters galore. They have also been featured on lots of general-interest magazines like *People* and *Us*. There are books, authorized and unauthorized (this is one of the latter), and there will be novelizations—book-length versions of some of the shows' episodes and of original stories written strictly for books. For some popular TV shows, like "Star Trek," there have been more adventures in novelizations than in the actual series.

All this merchandising is pure gravy. Right now the real money is going to come from selling advertising on the show. That's one of the reasons demographic studies are so important. When an advertising agency gets ready to plunk down a few hundred thousand dollars for a few seconds of airtime the agency wants to be pretty darn sure it will be reaching the sort of people who will buy the product being advertised. It would be a waste of money to try to sell denture adhesives on "90210," for example, and Clearasil would not find many takers among the millions who watch "Golden Girls."

In advertising, raw numbers are not everything. Advertisers do not like to pay to reach people who haven't the faintest interest in their product. "Beverly Hills, 90210" has a large and well-defined audience. Anything that appeals to teens, from jeans to audiotapes to teen-oriented films will do well to advertise on this show. Denture adhesives will be hawked elsewhere.

There is also the matter of credibility and identification. "Beverly Hills, 90210" is not a show you watch passively. You love the kids at West Beverly High. You identify with them, with their triumphs and tragedies, likes and dislikes. You are far more likely to want to buy something that is connected with them. Advertisers know that and are willing to pay to have their product displayed on such a show.

And then there are your parents. "Beverly Hills, 90210" is not a show for parents. Your folks probably won't watch it. Would you want them seated beside you while you watch? Somehow I doubt that you would. They might not even like the show. But it's not their show. It's not their world. It's your show. It's your world. However, your parents are probably not going to hate the show, either. And for advertisers that's important.

I hesitate to say that the show is considered respectable by adults, because statements like that are usually a big turnoff for teens. But it is considered respectable. Sure, there are those who believe that any discussion of teen sex will put you on the fast track to eternal damnation. Those people probably think the show is too loose morally. Dylan can get drunk and not be immediately punished by being crushed to death in a horrible auto accident. Some adults might regard his survival as a message that encourages teen drinking. But, by and large, the show promotes solid values—the sort of values the understanding and tolerant Walshes would favor, not the values of the Cleaver family of the 1950s, but that was an unreal world anyway. A lot has changed since "Leave It to Beaver."

So while your folks are probably not going to watch the show with you every Thursday night, they probably won't object to your seeing it. "Beverly Hills, 90210" is not as "dangerous" as Madonna's latest performance on HBO.

Respectability (sorry to keep using the word, but that's what it is) promotes peace in the home and creates a feeling of well-being among the advertisers. If parents, who in the end control the money for most teens, really object to a show they are also going to object to shelling out money for products connected with something they disapprove of. Advertisers know that as well. Parents are more likely to find many of the ads, like a recent one for No Excuses jeans featuring a well-known and controversial tennis champion, far more objectionable than the show on which it was aired.

Along with its enormous popularity, the producers of this show tout its respectability. Here's how they put in one of their promotion sheets: "Each episode deals with the social problems of teenagers head on in meaningful and socially responsible ways. The series has already won the Entertainment Industry Council Award as part of The Partnership for Drug Free America for an episode involving an alcoholic mother."

Teen-oriented shows are usually denounced by adults as socially irresponsible or just plain stupid. "Beverly Hills, 90210" is neither. It can enthrall millions of teens without driving their parents up the wall and making them threaten to shut off the electricity on Thursday evenings.

Now all of this may not mean a great deal to you. You're probably not interested in marketing, demographics, novelizations, and the rest. You want to know what's going to happen to Brandon and Brenda and Dylan and the others at West Beverly High.

But it is something that real fans should know about. In the end television is about making money—lots of money. If a show doesn't make lots of money, then no matter how much you love it, no matter how good or how significant it is, it's going to disappear. Perhaps that's not the way it should be, but that's the way it is in the real world of television.

Right now, looking at the hard and cold dollars-and-cents figures for "Beverly Hills, 90210," it is safe to predict that it will be around for a long time. So you can relax, sit back, enjoy, and identify with the goings-on at West Beverly High. There may be troubles on campus and in the personal lives of the students, but in the accounting offices of the TV executives, you'll see nothing but broad smiles, and those who watch the bottom line are going to make darn sure that the kids at West Beverly will be around for a long time to come.

If things keep going the way they have been, these students may have the longest high school careers in history. And that, too, means money above and beyond what is made on the show itself. Once a show is popular and has run for a certain length of time, it goes into syndication. This means that reruns will be shown on independent channels. Once again, "Star Trek" is the prime example. No matter where you live, you can almost certainly find reruns of that show on some channel at some time. Now, remember that show only lasted three seasons, but it has been in reruns forever. You can also find episodes of "I Love Lucy" and "The Honeymooners" being rerun regularly, even though they were made during the old days of black-and-white television. These shows and many like them have made far more money in reruns than they ever did originally. Syndication is an enormous business, and many TV executives claim that the real money is in syndication. In two or three years you will be able to watch Brandon and Brenda's first days at West Beverly running on an independent channel one night while their new and continuing adventures are aired once a week on the Fox network.

Will there be a *Beverly Hills, 90210: The Movie*? No one has said anything yet, and not all successful TV series have done well when transferred to the big screen. But surely the powers who run this show must be thinking about a film.

How about the rest of the world? Another big part of the TV business is selling U.S. programs abroad. Most of the TV sets that we watch were made in Japan and South Korea. But the most popular TV programs in the world are made right here in the United States. People in Hong Kong might not be able to locate Dallas on a map, but they sure can find it in their weekly TV schedule. Some U.S. shows "travel"—that is, become popular in other countries—and others don't. Occasionally a show that flopped in the United States will catch on abroad. After an initial burst of enthusiasm, "Twin Peaks" lost its American audience, but it became a huge hit in France. American movies depend heavily on selling to foreign markets to make a profit. U.S. television shows do not have to depend so heavily on foreign sales, but they don't scorn such sales, either.

Will a southern California zip code reach teens in Melbourne and Moscow? Who knows? Like betting on which new shows will succeed or fail, the experts are usually wrong about which series will travel well, and it's unwise to make predictions. But if "Beverly Hills, 90210" is reaching teens in Iowa and Georgia as well as in southern California, it must have a wide appeal. The show deals with universal themes in the lives of young people everywhere, and there is no reason why teens in Belgrade and

Berlin will not respond in much the same way as teens throughout the United States have. The series already appears to be a hit in Britain.

Don't you wonder what Dylan will sound like in Spanish?

4 ☆ Actors and Characters

☆
☆
☆
☆
☆
☆
☆

You know that there is no real West Beverly High and that the students there are not real high school students. They are professional actors. But in some instances, particularly in shows like "Beverly Hills, 90210" that are enormously popular and use actors who have not been well known for other parts, the identification between actor and character can be close. Too close for comfort in some cases. Yet the studios like to encourage this kind of identification because it makes the show seem more real.

One of the show's most closely guarded secrets is the real ages of the principal cast members. In the reams of material about the show issued by the Fox publicity depart-

ment you won't find any birthdays listed.
And in interviews most cast members de-
cline to directly answer the question "How
old are you?"

Keeping the ages of the actors a secret is a
harmless enough deception and a common
one. Acting is basically a business of illusion anyway. Jason Priestley, when avoid-
ing the question, has said that he doesn't
want to "spoil the illusion."

But illusion it is. The three principal cast
members—Jason Priestley, Shannen
Doherty, and Luke Perry—are well past
their teens. They would be the oldest kids in
any high school. Some of the other West
Beverly High "students" still are teens—but
just barely.

So let's destroy the illusion. How old *are*
the members of the West Beverly High
crowd?

Jason Priestley has been very evasive
about his age, and successfully so, though
he does admit that he is in his twenties—
twenty-four or twenty-five are the most
commonly reported ages. He is not at all shy
about giving his birth date. It's August
28—but in what year?

Shannen Doherty has been in show business for a long time. Of all the cast members she had the most successful career
prior to "90210." She has a reputation for

being outspoken. Besides, her biography was printed so many times before she joined the show that there is no point in her denying that she was born in 1971.

Luke Perry is not nearly as outspoken as Shannen. But he, too, has been acting for a long time, and biographical material was distributed by shows he had previously worked on. It says that he was born in 1966. Luke says he doesn't want his age to become an issue. As a professional he knows the difficulties of being a teenage actor. "It's hard to act that age when you are that age," he has said. "There's so much turbulence in your life at that time. It's easier and more convincing to play a seventeen- or eighteen-year-old when you're a few years older." As far as millions of teens are concerned, he's been giving a very convincing performance.

The cast member who is most open about her age is Tori Spelling, who plays Donna Martin. As the daughter of producer Aaron Spelling she would have found it impossible to hide her age. Besides she doesn't need to. She turned eighteen on her last birthday, May 16, 1991. As befits one of the stars of a hit show and the daughter of the producer, her eighteenth birthday party was a real show-biz production.

Jennie Garth (Kelly Taylor) is also a teenager, though just barely. She's nineteen.

Ian Ziering (Steve Sanders) acknowl-
edges that he graduated from William Paterson College in Wayne, New Jersey, with a
B.A. in dramatic arts. He is probably in his
mid-twenties.

Brian Austin Green (David Silver) will
qualify as a teenager for another year at
least. Last July 15 he turned eighteen.

The official biographies of the actors also
do not supply the ages of James Eckhouse
and Carol Potter who play Jim and Cindy
Walsh, Brandon and Brenda's parents. But
then, no one asked.

Smoking is something else that separates
the actors from the characters they play.
None of the major characters on the show
are smokers. Yet those who visit the set of
"Beverly Hills, 90210" acknowledge that
the smell of cigarette smoke is part of the
atmosphere.

Clean-cut Brandon Walsh wouldn't touch
a cigarette. Real-life Jason Priestley is a
heavy smoker. He doesn't say that smoking
is good for him, but he vigorously defends
his right to smoke if he wants to. "The thing
I hate most in the world," he says, "is
someone coming up to me and saying, 'Oh,
you shouldn't smoke. You're too young to
smoke.' It's none of your business."

Luke Perry and Tori Spelling are also smokers, though they don't make a big deal about their habit. They would not like to be regarded as role models for that part of their lives.

On the other side of the issue is Shannen Doherty, a militant nonsmoker. She was once a national youth ambassador for the American Lung Association and has done public service announcements and appearances publicizing the dangers of smoking. She thinks not smoking is everybody's business.

All of the principal players in "90210" emphasize that they are not the characters they portray. They may like some things about their characters and dislike others, but they don't want their fans to become confused between illusion and reality once the show is over. Still, it isn't easy to keep actor and character separate, particularly on a show like this, where the audience identifies so strongly and emotionally with the characters.

In the past actors have been trapped by typecasting. They may play one strong role early in their careers, and it makes such an impression that they are never able to successfully play anything else. There are hundreds of examples. Tony Perkins, a fine actor, will forever be the nutty Norman

Bates of *Psycho*. No matter how hard he tries, Christopher Reeve will always be Superman, and Sylvester Stallone has been trying to break the Rocky-Rambo mold for years, without much success.

Right now the young actors of "Beverly Hills, 90210" aren't worrying about future typecasting. They have great roles in a wildly successful show. They are on top of the world and still enjoying the view.

5 ☆ On the Set

We have just been talking about reality and illusion, the differences between the actors and the characters they play. Acting involves another type of illusion—the illusion that the actor's life is one of unrelieved glamour and fun.

Putting together a show like "Beverly Hills, 90210" week after week requires more hard work than glamour and fun. Oh, sure, it's more glamorous than flipping burgers at the local fast-food restaurant. The pay is better, too—lots better—but the hours are also longer.

You and I see the final result: one hour of entertainment a week. But putting that hour together took the whole week, sometimes every single day of the week, and sometimes as much as sixteen hours a day. Actors need a lot of stamina.

Television acting is hard work, and much of it is just plain boring. Actors spend a tremendous amount of time simply sitting around waiting to do a scene. And then they have to do it over if it isn't just right the first time. And then they do it over again, and again. They also have to go through make-up, costume changes, rehearsals, and hours and hours of learning lines. The young stars of "Beverly Hills, 90210" love their work and probably wouldn't trade it for any other job in the world right now. But it's still work.

And still speaking of illusion, the show is shot in southern California, but it isn't shot in Beverly Hills. The studio is in a couple of entirely different zip codes. Beverly Hills is just too expensive.

The bulk of the filming is done in the far less glamorous, and less expensive, town of Van Nuys in California's San Fernando Valley. There are sets for Brenda's room, the corridor of West Beverly High, the interior of the Peach Pit or wherever else the action is supposed to be taking place. Some of the exterior scenes are actually shot outside a high school in Orange County, but not in Beverly Hills. There are also some location shoots, at the beach or in episodes like the one in which the gang went camping in the mountains.

Aside from the sets and the actors who temporarily inhabit them, there is nothing at all glamorous about the Van Nuys studio. It looks like a collection of old warehouses, which in fact is exactly what it is.

Surrounding the studio is a high steel fence, meant to keep out the fans. The show's producers don't even like people to know the exact location of the studio. You can get in only with a special pass, and that pass is carefully examined by uniformed and very suspicious guards. The security is necessary. If a mob of fans can nearly trample Luke Perry at a shopping center, think what might happen at a studio. Even a small disruption could ruin hours of work, and like every weekly show "90210" runs on a very tight schedule. And then there is all that expensive equipment. This is not one of the many shows that are filmed live in front of a studio audience. Everyone on the set works there or has a special invitation.

Work starts early in the morning. How early depends on what has to be done. Top cast members Jason, Shannen, and Luke, who generally have the most scenes, work the longest days, often stretching into nights.

A sixteen-hour stretch on the set is not uncommon. And that sort of schedule can go on for several days running.

For the actors the day starts with "hair and makeup." In live theater most actors do their own makeup, but in films and TV this is in the hands of professionals who know what kind of makeup will look right for which lights and camera angles.

Then comes "wardrobe," where clothes are provided for each actor to wear. The off-screen Shannen does not dress like the on-screen Brenda, and the same is true for the rest of the actors. When the show first began, the producers had very tight control over what each character would wear. But as it has progressed and the actors have grown into their roles, they have been able to exercise greater choice over what they will wear during the show. Still, any radical change in style would have to get approval from the directors and producers. The proper image must be maintained.

For the most part, cast and crew are enthusiastic and almost joyful during the long hours of work. *Us* magazine calls the atmosphere on the "90210" set *"phenomenally* joyous. The actors joke and giggle with one another between takes; everybody walks around hugging and kissing."

The director, the magazine continues,

never raises his voice. If you have had any experience with directors at all, you will know that is phenomenal. Spirits are still high at ten o'clock on Friday night. The director quips, "All right, guys, tense up!"

Of course they *should* feel good, because the show and their careers are riding so very high. But once in a while the strain does show.

At one point Jason demanded that the set be cleared of all press people, and he refused to do any more interviews while other members of the cast were present. That bothered some of the cast members who played smaller roles, because they thought they weren't getting enough press coverage.

Jennie Garth (Kelly Taylor) almost collapsed on the set one day and was rushed to a hospital. It was just stress, and she was released after a brief examination.

And then there is Shannen. While she is by far the most experienced actor in the group, she is also, by reputation, the most "difficult." Her mood swings on the set have become legendary.

Other cast members are likely to ignore or laugh about the flubbed lines and dropped props that are part of filming every show, and there is even talk of a "Beverly Hills, 90210" gag reel, "Beverly Hills Bloopers," made up of the funniest flubs, but these little mistakes have been known to plunge Shannen into a deep depression or send her off the set in tears. When she comes back and the scene goes right, though, she can be laughing and hugging everyone in sight.

Between scenes she has been known to lock herself in her dressing room and play her stereo at a deafening volume.

Aaron Spelling, who has seen just about everything in the years he has spent producing TV shows, says, "She does some strange things."

On screen, Luke Perry looks relaxed and laid back, but while working he is focused and extremely intense. He is very, very serious about his work. "The only thing I know how to do besides act is physical labor," he has said. "I was a paver, I was a cook, I drove people around in their Mercedes, I worked in a video store, I sold shoes, I worked in a hotel. . . . When I think of the alternatives . . . my alternatives are not pleasant."

Jason, on the other hand, does not seem to be serious about anything. He is completely professional when the camera rolls. He likes to get his work done fast. If he can't nail a scene in two or three takes he gets impatient. Between takes he keeps everybody loose.

Aaron Spelling loves him because he

makes life on the set easier for everyone. "Jason's been our quarterback, keeping everyone on an even keel."

Still, some on the set are quick to point out that Jason also spends a lot of time on the phone with his business agent. He is not just living for the moment.

The funniest guy on the set is Brian Austin Green. His fellow actors describe him as the class clown. He's the guy who brings high-powered water pistols to work— and uses them.

Ian Ziering (Steve Sanders), on the other hand, is more of a stand-up comic. To get people to laugh he relies on jokes rather than gimmicks or stunts.

There is no commissary at the studio. All the food is prepared by caterers and trucked in. Most of the cast will take whatever is offered, though what is offered is a lot better than what you are likely to find on the steam table in your school lunchroom. Shannen, always the individualist, generally orders separately. She's not a health-food nut, but she prefers to "eat healthy" and limits red meat.

There are fights, tension, jealousy, and resentment on the set of "Beverly Hills, 90210." The actors are, after all, human. But considering the strain under which they habitually work, this is a remarkably friendly and together bunch. On a lot of other shows, some cast members won't even speak to one another unless the lines are in the script, and they spend most of their off-camera time cutting one another up. That doesn't happen on this set.

Still, mixed in with the obvious enthusiasm and good feeling there is a bit of nervousness and anxiety. Things have happened so fast and their success has been so massive that the actors worry about not being able to handle it. Since no one knows exactly why the show has worked so well, there is an almost superstitious fear that all the attention might break the spell and ruin the magic formula. Gabrielle Carteris (Andrea Zuckerman) summed up the fear for reporter Karen Schoemer: "We are at a time that could really make or break the show. I think everybody thinks that we've made it, because we're in our second season and there's so much response. And it's exciting and it's scary because it's new for all of us."

6 ☆ Jason Priestley/ Brandon Walsh

Brandon Walsh is a somewhat naive West Beverly High transfer student from Minneapolis.

Jason Priestley, the actor who plays Brandon, wasn't born in Beverly Hills, either. And that's just about where the similarity between character and actor ends.

Jason was born and raised in Vancouver, British Columbia, the westernmost province of Canada. An old show-biz expression, "born in a trunk," describes the children of vaudevillians. Their parents traveled so much that the children might really be born and raised backstage. Jason wasn't quite born in a trunk, but he did come from a show-business family.

His grandfather was a circus acrobat, his older sister an actress and model, and his father a one-time set builder. His mother, who performed under the professional name Sharon Kirk, was Canada's leading ballerina until a leg injury cut her dancing career short. Jason notes with pride that she gave two command performances for the queen of England.

Sharon Kirk was also a choreographer, singer, and actress. In Jason's first professional role he played a three-month-old baby; that was typecasting, since he *was* a three-month-old baby. He didn't really get serious about acting until he was much older—four, to be exact.

Cute, blue-eyed, fair-haired little Jason began appearing in local TV commercials. He insists that he was not pushed into a show-business career by an ambitious stage mother. Quite the reverse. His mother had serious reservations about dragging him from one audition to another. As an experienced performer herself, she had seen just how damaging such an experience could be to some youngsters. It was Jason who was the pushy one. He wanted to go to the auditions; he wanted to get an agent. Even at the age of four he loved to perform in front of a camera. He thrived on the attention.

Local ads led to national ads and to small parts in Canadian sitcoms and other TV shows. He enrolled in drama classes and at the age of eight got his first major role in a Canadian TV movie called *Stacey*. At an early age he learned some hard truths about the acting business: you have to show up on time, be prepared, and be ready to take direction and rejection; and even the best actors don't get all the parts they try out for. "If you can't take rejection, don't be an actor," he says.

Jason's career was going well, but the acting jobs were still only occasional; there was no time-consuming continuing role in a series or play. He didn't have to go to school on the set, as so many young actors do. So Jason had a relatively normal childhood. He didn't grow up entirely surrounded by other young actors and isolated from the rest of the kids his own age. He describes himself at that time of his life as "Joe Average."

It sounds like an almost idyllic childhood. But it wasn't for Jason Priestley. Instead of making him a hero at his school, his acting made him a pariah, an outsider. There were lots of nasty comments: "Hey, I saw you on TV last night, and you had lipstick on." There was also name-calling, and it hurt. Jason's classmates were jealous, and they really didn't understand what actors do. But it hurt nonetheless.

There were professional strains as well. Jason was no longer a little kid, and he couldn't get little-kid parts. He was growing into a teenager, and there were fewer opportunities in commercials and very few parts for teens in sitcoms. He had to work harder to get a job. This crisis is faced by many, many actors who began as children and had early success. Some are able, after a few rocky years, to make the transition to older roles. Many can't and simply drop out of the business forever. For a while it was not clear what would happen to Jason.

Then there were the inevitable strains and pressures of just growing up. With all of this, he rebelled against his family's show-business background and against his own budding acting career.

This was about 1980. Jason adopted the punk style. He wore heavy boots and chains, and he shaved his hair into the Mohawk style. There were not many parts open for young actors with Mohawks. This rebellion nearly cost Jason his career, and that's just what he intended. "I wanted to be a kid, and I was a kid."

If he had tried out for "Beverly Hills, 90210" during those rebellious years he would probably have been cast in the role of

Dylan, the brooding outsider rather than the sweet and sincere Brandon. But at that moment he wasn't trying out for anything. Of this time in his life he says he was "a rebel without a clue."

There is, however, a saying about acting: "It gets in the blood." No matter what else you're going through in your life, you don't give up the desire to act. While Jason had stopped actively pursuing acting jobs, he was still attending acting classes, still perfecting his craft. He had to sharpen his skills, because he couldn't get along just by being a cute kid anymore.

By the age of sixteen, the active stage of his rebellion was over. He was out looking for acting jobs again. And this good-looking, talented, and newly focused young man began finding them. While still living in Vancouver he got roles in the TV series "Danger Bay" and "MacGyver" and in the TV films *Lies from Lotusland* and *Nobody's Child*. There were also a couple of Canadian films, *Caddo Lake* and *Watchers*. He appeared on stage in productions of *The Breakfast Club*, *Rebel Without a Cause*, and *Addict*.

Jason also landed a couple of appearances on the hit Fox teenage series "21 Jump Street," which was shot in Vancouver. He wasn't doing clean-cut roles then.

He had a recurring part as a tough teen named Tober. The next season he played an alcoholic. "I used to play bad guys," he said. "I used to play really hard bad guys." These parts got him noticed in California, where most TV shows are made.

Vancouver is a lovely city, but it is not really a center for TV or films. Canada is not really a center for TV or films. As his career blossomed, Jason began commuting between Vancouver and Los Angeles. The pace, however, was too grueling, and by the age of eighteen he had decided to relocate to Los Angeles more or less permanently, although he is still a Canadian citizen. It was a radical move, because Los Angeles is very different from Vancouver. It was a little bit like moving from Minnesota to Beverly Hills. Jason, however, says that he was a good deal more experienced and worldly than Brandon Walsh.

His parents were very supportive of the move, and Jason had enough money from his previous acting jobs to keep going until he found work in L.A. He never set a time limit for himself.

"I knew what I wanted to do," he said, "and I knew it would take time; everything takes time. John Cassavetes [a fine actor and director] always said, 'Everybody gets a shot, and most people don't wait around long enough to get it.' Those are the words I have lived by. I never nearly gave up. I knew that I had to keep slugging away, keep doing it."

Jason Priestley wasn't an overnight success, but he didn't have to wait too long. While the work didn't exactly pour in the moment he moved to California, he received more than enough offers to keep him off the soup line.

He appeared in "Airwolf II" and the popular "Quantum Leap," where he played a gang member. He did, however, get a couple of fairly clean-cut, albeit small, roles in Disney Channel movies. Later the Disney folks gave him starring roles in *Teen Angel* and the sequel, *Teen Angel Returns*.

What looked like Jason Priestley's big break came when he was tapped to costar with veteran actress Stephanie Beacham in the series "Sister Kate." She played a tough-as-nails nun who ran an orphanage, and Jason played Todd Mahaffey, the eldest and probably the dumbest of the orphans. According to the network's official description of the character he is "Street smart, but not as smart as he thinks he is." Jason's description of the character is a little harsher: "He had the IQ of a bag of dirt."

Still, it was a regular job on a major American TV show. It could have turned him into a major teen idol, if the show had lasted. But it didn't last. After the debut of "Sister Kate" in September 1989, the critics panned it. Unlike the later experience with "Beverly Hills, 90210," the public didn't pick up on it. And within a few months "Sister Kate" was gone.

The loss was depressing for Jason. But he was already experienced in show business. He knew things like this happened all the time, and he was ready for it. Besides, he had never really liked the character anyway. "Todd was a pretty one-dimensional character. There wasn't much going on inside him."

Jason wasn't out of work for long. In the spring of 1990 producer Aaron Spelling was putting together the cast for what was then called "Class of Beverly Hills." The plot centered on a set of twins from Minnesota who found themselves amid the sun and palms of fast and ritzy Beverly Hills. Most of the cast had already been signed, but there was still one big hole. Someone was needed to play the male half of the twins. He had to be clean-cut and sincere, with solid moral values, and above all, he had to be real.

Spelling's daughter, Tori, who had already won herself a spot on the new show, remembered seeing Jason in "Sister Kate." The rather dull-witted Todd character was not at all like the character projected for Brandon, who was to be a tower of good sense and sanity. Yet Tori liked the actor's looks, and she saw possibilities. Growing up in the home of one of TV's most successful producers had apparently given her an eye for picking actors.

Tori told her dad. He listened. Jason was called in for an audition, and he got the part. He was delighted, naturally, but even in his most optimistic moments it is doubtful if he realized what it would lead to. At that time, nobody did.

Jason had always hoped for a big success: "You have to set your goals and your aspirations so high that you will probably never attain them. So you set them high, and if you do attain it, then you set one even higher to go for."

His first goal as an actor, he says, was just to keep working. He has certainly attained that goal: "Then when you start working you say, 'Okay, now I need to really do something that I think is really good and something I could be proud of.'"

Jason Priestley isn't Brandon Walsh. He doesn't pretend to be, except when he is playing the part. Off-screen he doesn't even look that much like Brandon. But he is constantly asked about the character of Brandon and how he sees him. And he has contributed to the development of the character in the series. He doesn't see Brandon as completely innocent or naive. In fact, as the show has progressed, the character of Brandon had become more sophisticated, worldly, and self-assured. The keys to the character, says Priestley, are his core of basic and solid values and his good sense. He makes mistakes, of course, but he's basically sound.

Brandon is far from perfect. Says Jason, "Brandon's got a bad side. We just haven't seen it yet. We saw a little of it when he got drunk and crashed the car. There's more." Can we expect any major character shift in Brandon Walsh? Don't bet on it. We may see more of his feet of clay, but there isn't likely to be the kind of complete turnaround that is common on soap operas and in professional wrestling. Brandon Walsh is going to remain basically a good guy. There is a very popular saying, "If it ain't broke, don't fix it." This show ain't broke, and no one is going to tamper with the very delicate formula for success that "90210" has found.

There are pitfalls in playing the good guy. Any actor will tell you the villain's part is usually better. In fact, there is an old theater proverb: "The snake has all the good lines." The problem with the Brandon character is that he might come across as *too* good. He could look smug and self-righteous. That would make the character even less popular than all the punks and tough guys that Jason used to play, and it would hurt the show. No one, particularly no teen, wants to be lectured.

Time and again Jason has insisted that he does not wish to sound preachy. He has said that so often that "Priestley not Preachy" has become a catchphrase used by many fan magazines. The fact that he has been able to pull off this difficult feat is a tribute to his abilities as an actor.

He also credits his family. His father had a way of telling him things without being preachy. Jason remembers when he was in high school and the subject of drinking came up. He remembers his father saying to him, "'Jason, if you go out and have a few drinks, that's fine. I know sometime you're going to do it, but whatever you do, don't get in a car. Give me a call and I'll come and pick you up.' That's the kind of relationship we have. I don't know if everyone's relationship with their father is like that."

This is the tone adopted by the entire show. Says Jason: "Some kids are going to experiment. The only thing you can do is educate them and say, 'Look, if you drink, don't do this or don't do that.' What happens after that is a matter of individual responsibility."

On the set, Jason is one of the most relaxed and easygoing of the cast members. Off the set, he continues his Canadian heritage by playing hockey. He plays center on a division two hockey team competing against NFL veterans across the country. One of his teammates is Michael J. Fox. Jason is also a devotee of some other tough sports like rugby, motorcycling, and skiing. He has recently taken up a new craze—bungee jumping. "Oh, God, I just willingly committed suicide," he jokes. This hobby doubtless sends network executives racing for the antacid as they watch their newest and hottest property throw himself off a bridge, protected only by a harness and a flexible rope. He has gentler pursuits as well—golf, tennis, and just hanging out.

But still, acting and show business in general are the main interests in Jason Priestley's life. One of his heroes is Cary Grant, another actor who radiated easy charm.

"I always loved Cary Grant," Jason says. "Cary Grant was probably the only actor of that time that wasn't afraid to make a real idiot of himself for the sake of the part that he was doing. He was like the bumbling idiot most of the time. If you look at him in *Arsenic and Old Lace,* he was insane; he was great. And Humphrey Bogart, too. Humphrey is cool. . . . It's almost like Cary Grant—he could say, 'Forget it. I'm going to be this wild, goofy character!' Probably some people would have a problem with that."

As for the future, Jason talks about the possibility of directing and scriptwriting. "I don't think I'm a very good writer," he has said, but he does contribute script ideas to the show. Still, he notes, realistically, "I have to master one craft before going on to another."

And for all his cool, the sudden fame has clearly made him a little uncomfortable. The press and his fans ask him all sorts of serious questions. He tries to turn them aside with humor. It's like he's saying, "Hey, guys, I'm just one very lucky actor. I don't know all those other things."

7 ☆ Shannen Doherty/ Brenda Walsh

There is an irony in the "Beverly Hills, 90210" scripts: Brenda Walsh is an aspiring acress who saves her money for acting lessons.

Shannen Doherty, who plays Brenda, however, is undoubtedly the most experienced actor among the younger cast members. She didn't start as an infant and come from a show-business family, as did Jason Priestley, but she did start very young and had by far the greatest success of any of the "90210" cast prior to joining the show. She was the only one with an established name, the only one who had been a star of a TV series—two of them, in fact. She also starred in a movie that has attained cult status. Of all the "90210" cast she is probably the most serious, and the most sensitive about her acting.

One of Shannen's celebrated blowups came while filming a scene about a summer drama class in which Brenda was enrolled. The subject of the class was Shakespeare, and Brenda had to do part of a scene. She flubbed the lines several times, and finally became so frustrated that she ran off the set.

The situation was resolved after a while, and filming continued. The next day Shannen explained: "It was the Shakespeare. I always know my lines. . . . I was in front of a crowd performing something I wasn't very familiar with. I've read Shakespeare, but I've never actually performed it before. So it's all very new to me. I got hot out there, and I just got very nervous, and then I couldn't get it straight. Also, when I screw up I get really mad at myself. So it was like a whole emotional breakdown that happened."

Chuck Braverman, one of the show's directors, is also known as "Shannen's director." He takes a lot of time with her and understands her best. He is very patient with her, and after some rocky moments when the show began, the two now get along.

Jason Priestley and Luke Perry hit the beach between scenes. . . . © **Michael Grecco/Outline Press**

Shannen Doherty poses between her two hot costars backstage at the 43rd Annual Emmy Awards in Los Angeles.

© Vincent Zuffante/STAR FILE PHOTO

SHANNEN

Talking with Tori . . .

. . . and gabbing with Gabrielle

© 1990 Heidi Gibbs/VISAGES

JASON

An unforgettable couple: Jennie Garth and Ian Ziering © Vincent Zuffante/STAR FILE PHOTO

LUKE

Brian Green, Luke, and Jason go to bat for the T. J. Martell Foundation celebrity softball game. © ARCHIVE PHOTOS/Darlene Hammond

"Shannen and I have become closer and closer on each show," he says. "She's a very strong-willed woman. She used to disagree with me more when I would make a suggestion. Now she listens to me, and more often than not she'll take it. One of the things I've done with Shannen is to try to soften her character and make her more vulnerable. I think it's because I'm really crazy about her and I don't want her to be the bad girl of '90210.'"

Shannen Doherty was born on April 12, 1971, in Memphis, Tennessee, the site of Elvis Presley's mansion, Graceland. She and her older brother Sean—the genius of the family, according to Shannen—spent their early years in Memphis. Then, when she was six, the family moved to Palos Verdes, a suburb of Los Angeles. Her father was a hard-driving banker until a serious stroke forced him to slow down. Her mother runs a facial salon now that she no longer has to accompany her precocious daughter to the studio every day.

Shannen's direction in life changed when she was eight and a friend asked her to watch an audition for a children's production of *Snow White*, which was to be done in a church. Shannen had never thought about acting before, but when she was invited to step up and try, she did. And she landed one of the leading parts. From that point on, she never looked back.

Her performance in *Snow White* attracted some local attention, and a well-meaning newspaper reporter suggested that she go to Los Angeles and try to find an agent. This suggestion did not sit well with Shannen's conventional parents. They had heard all sorts of terrible things about child actors and the way they lived. They wanted no part of it for their daughter.

At this point Shannen showed some of the determination that has since made her famous, and a bit infamous with her co-workers. She pestered her parents for two solid years until her mother finally took her to see some theatrical agents. Not only did she get an agent—within a week she got a job! It was a voice-over for the animated feature *The Secret of NIMH*. Then came commercials.

One year after her career started, she got her first TV role in a two-part episode of the series "Father Murphy." Her performance impressed the show's creator, the late Michael Landon. The following year Landon was putting together a sequel to the popular "Little House on the Prairie." The new NBC series was to be called "Little House: A New Beginning." Landon personally picked Shannen to play Jenny Wilder. Working full-time on a TV series altered Shannen's life drastically. In fact, it changed the life of the entire Doherty family.

Shannen's mother, Rosa, came to the set every day to make sure that her little girl wasn't being overworked and that she got three hours of on-set schooling every day. Shannen had always been a good student, and even though she was now a working acress, her academic success didn't suffer.

"Little House: A New Beginning" didn't last long. Within a year Shannen was looking for work—and finding it.

She had guest roles on such shows as "21 Jump Street," "Life Goes On," "Magnum, P.I.," "The Outlaws," "Airwolf," and "The Voyagers." She also starred with Lindsay Wagner and Jack Scalia in the TV movie *The Other Lover* and with Brad Davis and Jack Warden in the TV miniseries *Robert Kennedy and His Times*. She even did a turn on the trapeze in the celebrity show-off production "Circus of the Stars."

Though television has always been her main arena, Shannen also ventured into feature films. She had a small role in *Night Shift* and a bigger one in *Girls Just Want to Have Fun*. She also made an appearance in something called *The Treasury of Green Piney*. But far and away her best feature film role was in the black comedy *Heathers*, which didn't make much of an impact on the big screen but has gone on to become something of a teen cult film on TV and videotape. She starred as Heather Duke, the dominating beauty among four high school girls named Heather. Her costars in the film were some of the hottest young actors in Hollywood: Christian Slater, Winona Ryder, Lisanne Falk, and Kim Walker. Heather Duke is a role Shannen Doherty fans will always remember.

With all this activity Shannen and her agent were still looking around for a new TV series. Some actors don't like series, but Shannen says that she has always enjoyed the security and family feeling of working with the same cast and crew week after week instead of having to get used to an entirely new group on every job. In 1986 she found that new series. It was another house —"Our House," also on NBC.

The series starred lovable old Wilford Brimley, now best known for his Quaker Oats commercials. In that series a widow and her three children suddenly came to live with the woman's father-in-law (Brimley). It was the sort of show that is supposed to be heartwarming. Shannen played Kris Witherspoon, the middle daughter. The character was strong, warm, and very opinionated, not unlike Shannen herself.

While being interviewed about that show, Shannen said: "The producers have allowed me to develop my character according to what I feel and the things I'm comfortable with. That's why we're so much alike."

During the three years she spent with "Our House" Shannen began to develop her reputation for being difficult. Though she was only a teenager, she had very definite ideas about what her character should be like. And she was popular enough with the viewers to be able to say what she liked, whether the producers liked it or not, and get away with it. Difficult actors and actresses don't last long unless they are considered indispensable to a show.

Shannen knew how popular the character of Kris Witherspoon was, and she took her position as a role model very seriously. When one episode featured teenage Kris getting drunk and enjoying it, Shannen objected very loudly and very publicly. She didn't think that set a good example. So the script was changed: Kris wound up depressed after her drinking. Shannen also didn't want to have Kris yelling at her grandfather, because that showed disrespect for elders; so that script, too, was modified. There were other arguments as well. Shannen didn't win them all, but she didn't lose too many.

Shannen still takes her position as a role model very seriously. That's why she's such a militant nonsmoker. And though she loves the show, she is sometimes just a bit uncomfortable with the more hard-hitting themes.

While doing "Our House" Shannen also tried to live a normal life. In ninth grade she enrolled in a parochial school near her home. There were all the usual problems of being in a new school, but there was one much bigger problem: because of her demanding shooting schedule she wasn't in school that much. Though, as always, she kept up with her work, she felt the teachers resented her for not being in class, and the other students were both resentful and jealous. Sometimes it isn't easy being a TV star—or going to school with one. It was the most miserable school year of her life.

A year later she was attending an exclusive private school, where the headmistress understood the difficulties of a show-business life. In case you're thinking this was some Mickey Mouse school for spoiled-brat kid actors, it wasn't. The school was called the Lycée Français, and it's known as one of the most academically demanding schools in the country. It's Jodie Foster's alma mater, and she's considered one of the brainiest actors in the business.

With everything else that was going on in her life, Shannen still managed to maintain a 4.0 grade average and could have had her pick of colleges. Instead, she went back to high school—West Beverly High. But that didn't happen immediately.

"Our House" lasted three years—not bad for a TV series. Shannen was disappointed when it was canceled. She thought it could have gone on for another year. But at that point she picked up the role in *Heathers,* and her career was really hot. She got plenty of TV offers, for that was and is the medium in which she is best known, but she turned most of them down because she didn't like the roles she was being offered. She was getting stupid-teenager roles, and she resented them. She was looking for a part and a show with some substance.

"I don't like playing airheads," she says. "Anything that's demeaning to women, I don't want to do. If I'm going to play a teenager, I'm going to play someone with brains, intelligence—a thinking young person." As you might imagine, Shannen is very strong and unusually outspoken on women's issues.

When she was asked to audition for what

was still called "The Class of Beverly Hills," she read the script and jumped at the chance. Here was a show that didn't make kids look like a bunch of happy-go-lucky idiots. "It's very honest," she says. "It shows that teenagers do have values and morals." Naturally she got the part.

As with "Our House," Shannen takes herself and the show very seriously. In contrast to the laid-back Jason, she does preach: "We have a responsibility to our viewers to put out a positive message. None of us wants to put dirt on the air and let people watch that, because we're their role models in a way."

Shannen also takes her fan mail very seriously. She gets stacks of it, and of course she hasn't the time to answer it or even to read every letter personally. But she claims that she does answer some of the letters.

In addition to the simple fan letters a lot of kids write to "Brenda" for advice. Many of the questions they ask are about sex. Her advice on the subject can be summed up in five words: "Slow down and be careful."

Does Shannen identify with the character she plays? In a way, she does: "In the beginning we had nothing in common. [Brenda] was very insecure, would have done anything to be part of the clique. But she's maturing now, starting to realize some things . . . like she doesn't need a boyfriend for her life to be perfect, that she needs to stand on her own and find out who she is. That's an important lesson for any girl at any age."

Like the other lead actors on "Beverly Hills, 90210," Shannen increasingly has an opportunity to shape and direct the role she plays. You can expect to see Brenda become more opinionated and difficult, but more self-assured as well. She definitely does not want to become the bad girl of the series. Actually Shannen denies the rumors that she is difficult to work with, but her blow-ups on the set have been witnessed by too many to make total denial credible. Certainly one of the reasons for her displays of emotion is that she works so hard and puts everything into her performance. Reporter Lisa Schwarzbaum, while interviewing Shannen, noticed "a sleep-deprived pallor beneath her Brenda makeup."

If the grueling schedule is too much for Shannen, she doesn't seem to want it to stop. If she gets any interesting movie offers, she hopes she will be able to fit them into her schedule somehow. Shannen hopes "90210" will go on for years and years, and she thinks it's just going to get better.

"I just hope that the popularity doesn't

change us in any way," she has said. "Because we all want to be popular, and we all want the show to really take off, because it is a really good show. Give us a couple of years and let us establish our audience, and I think we will easily be in the top twenty." The way the show is going right now, it may not take a couple of years.

"So it's good," she continues. "It's just you can't let it affect you. In some ways it does change, the popularity does change it, but you can't all of a sudden think you can go out and do anything you want because you're a little bit famous."

Shannen Doherty may be more driven, more emotional, than many of the show's other cast members. But, though young, she is also a seasoned actress who has had success before "90210." Being a celebrity is not an entirely new experience for her. Despite an occasional blowup she may handle the success better than others.

She can even envision life after West Beverly High. She wants to be a producer so that she can create her own quality shows. And a family? Yes, that, too. With five kids.

Right now, though, Shannen lives alone in a house in the exclusive Malibu Beach area. Like the other stars of this show she is cautious about giving an exact address. Do remember that the word "fan" comes from "*fan*atic." In what little free time she has, she does a lot of exercising—"I try to stay in shape," she says. She also plays tennis and rides horses. She used to own a horse, but admits that she simply hasn't time to take care of one anymore.

All in all, Shannen Doherty is a remarkable young woman. She has been directing her own life since she was only ten—and very successfully, too. Sure, she may be difficult and opinionated, but she is also intelligent, extremely determined, and one fine actress. She has made the character of Brenda Walsh real, and a real idol to millions.

Director Chuck Braverman isn't the only one who's crazy about her.

8 ☆ Luke Perry/ Dylan McKay

Let's get the important facts out of the way first. Yes, Luke Perry is the one with the pet pig. The pig is named Jerry Lee, and Luke refers to it as his roommate. Jerry Lee is not one of those three-hundred-pound farm pigs. It's a Vietnamese potbellied pig—a miniature pig about the size of a beagle, but of course much fatter. It has short black hair and a curly tail, which it wags a lot, and it is very friendly and quite clean—for a pig. Potbellied pigs can be trained to use a litter box, just like cats. They are also one of the country's hot new pets, so keeping one in your apartment is not nearly as weird as it sounds. Now you know.

Luke Perry comes from Fredericktown,

Ohio. His father is a farmer, though like many family farmers today he had to take on an extra job in order to keep the farm going. In the case of Luke's father the job was in construction.

Luke does come from an essentially rural background. Where else in America are kids named Luke? Certainly not in Beverly Hills. And he likes to play up the farm background while the network publicists portray him as just "a skinny kid from Ohio" who still drives a ten-year-old pickup truck and drinks beer from the can. But Luke was not your average farm boy. In fact he didn't like the farm one little bit. From the moment he first began watching television he wanted to be an actor.

He says that he was about four years old when he saw the Paul Newman film *Cool Hand Luke* on TV. "I saw my name on TV," he once said. "I saw 'Luke' on TV. I'd never seen it written before. Then I watched the movie. After that I couldn't imagine my life being about anything else. I couldn't imagine not being an actor." He can't imagine why everybody doesn't want to be an actor.

However, acting is not a popular career choice for most of the kids in Fredericktown, and it wasn't easy wanting to be an actor in a town where everybody else wanted to be a farmer. During high school Luke kept his ambition pretty much to himself, for fear of being ridiculed. Though he tends to play it down in his interviews, the fact that he was not happy in Ohio quickly comes across.

In school he was bored and rebellious, like many of his classmates: "By the time I was in ninth grade the material that we covered in school all seemed very redundant to me. We were doing the same things over and over, which kind of put me at odds with a lot of my teachers, and no teacher wants to be second-in-command in their own classroom. . . . There were somewhat adversarial relationships there sometimes."

The casual observer might have assumed that the teenage Luke Perry, who played baseball, hung out with the guys, and watched a lot of TV, would wind up on the farm or in a factory somewhere. There was no way to measure his tremendous ambition or to predict the success he was to have.

When he graduated from high school, he didn't even bother to apply to college. "I didn't want to go to school anymore. I was sick of it."

He knocked around Ohio for a while, picking up odd jobs and trying somehow to get into acting. But there are few opportunities for aspiring actors in rural Ohio. "I was going nuts," Luke admits.

At the age of eighteen he decided to stop fooling around and really pursue his dream. Like so many other young people he moved to Los Angeles in order to be near the film and TV industries.

"Actually, I came out to L.A. to get warm," Luke quips. "I was sick of freezing my butt off in Ohio in the winter."

The boy from Ohio did not take Hollywood by storm. He enrolled in acting classes and was lucky enough to sign with an agent who got him to auditions. But an audition is not an offer, and it was three very tough years before Luke Perry began getting any viable acting offers.

In the meantime he had to eat and pay the rent, and he didn't have a rich family to support him through the lean years. "I worked on a factory assembly line making doorknobs, laid a lot of asphalt, painted parking lots, and even did some telephone sales," Luke said. "I did whatever it took to pay the rent."

Hollywood is one Mecca for actors; New York is the other. Since Hollywood didn't seem to be working out for him, Luke decided to try the other coast. He moved to New York.

Los Angeles—Hollywood in particular— is associated in the public mind with filmmaking and with television; New York is associated with the Broadway theater. In fact there is a great deal of TV shot in New York City. Several of the afternoon soap operas, for example, are shot there.

The soaps attract a lot of young actors, because they use—and use up—a lot of actors. But actors often have a rather snobbish attitude toward them. Even unemployed Luke Perry was resistant. "A lot of people are ashamed of them," he once said. "It's not something actors are proud of. I myself thought, Yes, of course I want to be an actor, but I don't want to do a soap opera."

But since Broadway producers were not flooding him with job offers, Luke swallowed his pride and auditioned for a soap. There were lots of actors reading for the part. One of them was a good-looking blond kid from New Jersey named Ian Ziering. At first Luke resented Ian because he already had a job on "Guiding Light" and merely wanted a better part. Luke, on the other hand, had no job at all. He wanted anything he could get. In the end, neither got the part. Ian went back to "Guiding Light," where his part was improved, and Luke went on to more auditions. Neither of them had any idea that they would eventually work together, but not in New York.

At one of the auditions for an ABC soap

opera called "Loving" Luke Perry got his first acting job. He played a character named Ned Bates, a role he wasn't crazy about. When Ned Bates was written out of the script, Luke went on to play Kenny in "Another World." Any snobbery that Luke had harbored about soap opera acting quickly evaporated. He realized just how demanding the work was. The shooting schedule is killing. New lines must be learned every day. The actors have to get it right the first time, for retakes are a luxury, and an actor who flubs too often will soon be out of a job.

"A certain performance level is expected out of you," says Luke. "It's like a big exam every day."

Though Luke did not become a soap opera star, for the former farm boy and parking-lot paver the pay was incredible. "I was rich," he says. "I made obscene money."

The good times lasted for about a year. Then the soap opera parts dried up. While waiting for another job, Luke did some commercials for Levi's jeans—he looks great in jeans—but the commercials also petered out after a while. Luke kept going to acting classes and trying out for just about everything that was offered. For a time nothing seemed to be breaking his way. "It was tough," he says. "But it made me an actor."

Things began to pick up when Luke landed a couple of off-Broadway roles. The off-Broadway theater didn't pay as well as the soaps, but it was work; it got him exposure. Then he played small roles in a couple of motion pictures. One of them, *Terminal Bliss*, Luke calls "Just a horrendous movie." Another film, *Scorchers*, gave him a chance to be in a cast that included Faye Dunaway and James Earl Jones. He loved working on that picture.

Luke Perry also loved New York. If he had been able to get regular work he probably would have stayed in the Big Apple. But an actor takes work where he can find it. And one day his agent called with news about a new show for teenagers that Aaron Spelling was producing for Fox. It was called "The Class of Beverly Hills."

He was told there was a part in the show that he might be just right for. The character was called Dylan McKay; it was a part that might once have appealed to the legendary James Dean. Dylan is rich, but totally alienated from his family and from all the trappings of wealth. He certainly doesn't look rich. One publication called the Dylan McKay character "a hood with a heart of gold." He is cool on the outside, but sensitive and more than a little troubled. And he's extremely bright, probably the most intellectual and the deepest of the West Beverly High crowd.

Though Luke considers himself almost totally unlike Dylan, he loved the part, particularly Dylan's intelligence. "I'm in awe of intelligent people. Before this, I never had the chance to play someone that smart. This is a dream role for me."

As you know, and every other teenager in America knows, Luke Perry did get the part, and he moved back to Los Angeles. As the show was originally conceived, the major characters were Brandon and Brenda. Dylan McKay was an interesting member of the supporting cast but not necessarily a major character. The size of his part was going to depend on how the audience responded, and boy, did the audience respond!

The one-time Ohio farm boy recently made *Us* magazine's list of the twenty sexiest men in the world. It is an honor he shares with fellow "90210" cast member Jason Priestley. Luke's fan mail is coming in at the rate of five hundred letters a week, and that figure is rising fast. When he arrived for a relatively unpublicized personal appearance at a Seattle area shopping mall early in the summer of 1991 there was a riot as five thousand screaming fans showed up instead of a few hundred, as anticipated. A thoroughly alarmed Luke Perry had to be smuggled out in a laundry hamper! There was an even wilder scene when he appeared at a south Florida shopping mall. This time ten thousand fans showed up. Security was better, but nevertheless, twenty-one people were injured. This is a promo stunt Luke will not repeat.

Dylan has become so popular that in the second season he may overshadow Brandon. He's a more complex and interesting character, and Luke's performance and rugged good looks have added to his popularity. But if there is any serious conflict between Jason Priestley and Luke Perry, it isn't apparent on the set.

Luke is more serious, but says that he and Jason have many similarities. "Know what you're doing, don't let anyone tell you anything different, have fun, and when the time comes, do your job," Luke says. "The work is very serious, and other than that—"

"Nothing is!" adds Jason.

Like Dylan McKay, Luke Perry tries to avoid the trappings of wealth and of his newfound fame. He lives in a modest house in what he calls a "low-rent" district of Hollywood. Don't ask for the address. He does drive a pickup truck, but it's not ten years old. In fact it's brand-new. He tries to keep his feet on the ground and will often tell interviewers that it took him over six years to become an "overnight success." He remembers the tough times and intends to work very hard to see that he doesn't have to go through them again.

Though Luke tends to be shy, he is far more outgoing, relaxed and friendly than the character he plays. He says he doesn't have Dylan's dark side. He doesn't surf, but he does play basketball. He also has a reputation as a pretty good cook.

What does Luke Perry see for the future?

"I had huge dreams, and I still have huge dreams," he said. "When I was watching the Academy Awards recently, I was seeing some of the great work that was being awarded. I have dreams of acting as well as Jeremy Irons [the fine English actor who took the Oscar for his role in *Reversal of Fortune*]. I do. I would be lying if I told you I didn't. We all do, but along with those dreams you have to have a dose of reality that says, 'Okay, it's fine to want to be that good, but this is how good you are at this point.' If you want to get from point A to Jeremy Irons, which is point B, it's going to require an awful lot of work. Only recently have I started to realize that. Now I am not so afraid to work hard, because I enjoy the work. I like the idea that over the next few years hopefully I will be given the opportunity to grow as a performer, and if I am wise, I will take advantage of it."

Beyond all the hype, and all the sex-symbol image-making is one very committed and very good actor.

9 ☆ Jennie Garth/ Kelly Taylor

Kelly Taylor is West Beverly High School's super-trendy rich kid. She sometimes seems spoiled, but there's a lot of heartache in her life. Her mother's an alcoholic. Her father has disappeared—no one seems to know where. She's had to grow up on her own.

Jennie Garth is playing against type. She grew up in Champaign-Urbana Illinois. The main campus of the University of Illinois is located there, but lots of farms surround the city. Jennie's parents were farmers, not academics. She spent many hours of her young life taking care of the farm animals, and the love for animals that developed at that time remains with her.

She's a big supporter of animal rights and a committed environmentalist.

Jennie's life as a farmer's daughter ended when she was thirteen. Her father became seriously ill, and the family had to move to a warmer and drier climate. Winters in central Illinois are damp and brutally cold. The family chose sunny Phoenix, Arizona.

If she had stayed on the farm in Illinois, Jennie would almost certainly never have become an actress. But Phoenix was a whole new world, and Jennie had trouble adjusting to it. In order to find something to do, she enrolled in a dance class—and found that she loved it and was good at it. She spent all her free time at the dance studio and even began teaching a class for younger students. At this point she was thinking of becoming a dancer.

By the time she was fourteen Jennie had blossomed into a real beauty, and she began making the rounds of some of the local beauty pageants. With her good looks and talent for dance, she did very well indeed. Beauty pageants have been the springboard for many aspiring actresses, and so it was for Jennie Garth.

She had already begun taking drama lessons from a former actress named Jean

Fowler, who thought she saw real potential in her student. "I knew this girl was going to be successful," she says. Still, it was a very long way from Phoenix beauty queen to actress—even to aspiring actress.

It was while Jennie was competing in a beauty pageant that she was approached by former ABC-TV casting director Randy James, and at this point she began taking the idea of an acting career seriously for the first time.

She didn't run off to Hollywood immediately. Her mother checked out James's credentials, because there are a lot of phonies, and worse, in the "talent" business. He was legitimate. Jennie continued her acting lessons and made tapes of her progress. These she sent to James, who offered invaluable criticism and advice. She was young and still unpolished, but she had a freshness and liveliness that really came across. After a few months James thought she was ready.

When the decision was finally made to go to Hollywood, Jennie didn't go alone. Her mother went with her. That meant splitting up the family for a while and giving up a successful real estate business, but Jennie's parents were supportive. They both had faith in their daughter's talent.

Randy James was now her agent, and

that gave Jennie a definite advantage over all those kids who show up in Hollywood without any connections at all. But still, it wasn't easy. She and her mother shared an apartment with three other people while they made the rounds of auditions, sometimes hitting as many as four a day. That's a grueling schedule, particularly if you don't get any jobs.

Jennie was beginning to think the decision to come to Hollywood was a mistake. Then, after four months, she finally got a part—a regular role in an NBC series called "A Brand New Life." The star was Barbara Eden, a veteran of other TV sitcoms. Jennie was fine, but the series wasn't. It lasted only seven episodes.

She got a few other minor parts, including one in the TV movie *Teen Angel Returns*. That's where she first met Jason Priestley, who played the starring role.

After having gone through so many auditions and gotten so few roles, Jennie was not overly optimistic about auditioning for the role of Kelly on "90210." She loved the part, but the character was so unlike her that she didn't think she stood a chance of winning it. But after her first audition she was called back, and then called back again and again. After four or five auditions she finally landed the part—to her surprise and ultimately to her delight.

"I'm proud to be on this show," she says. "It teaches kids that it's okay to make mistakes, and you don't have to grow up too quickly."

10 ☆ Ian Ziering/
Steve Sanders

There are two versions of how Ian (pro-
nounced EYE-an) Ziering got into show
business. Both of them begin in a supermarket in West Orange, New Jersey, where
Ian grew up. According to one version, at
the age of twelve he was spotted in the
supermarket by a talent agent who encouraged him go into show business.

The other version is less glamorous but
funnier. At the age of four he was in the
supermarket with his mother. In typical
high spirits, he was wrecking the place.
The supermarket manager came over to his
mother and told her she should channel the
active little boy's energies into something
more useful—like show business.

Whatever story you want to believe, Ian Ziering did go into show business when he was about twelve years old, though he was a show-off long before that.

He was an outgoing kid—"hyperactive" is one of the many words that have been used to describe him. He was always telling jokes and performing, but at first his mother, father, and two older brothers were his best and only audience. Then he began to appear in school plays, summer drama-camp productions, and community theater dramas.

Ian has dyslexia, which made schoolwork difficult for him. "It put a great damper on my academics," he said, "so I focused on creative things."

Though Ian is quite handsome now, he was a funny-looking kid: "I had adult teeth but not an adult head—so it was like I could chew apples through a picket fence."

By the age of twelve he had grown into his teeth, and talent agents did begin looking at him seriously. He signed up with a children's modeling agency and did a lot of print work as well as TV and radio commercials. More impressive was a part that he got in a movie. He played Brooke Shields's brother in *Endless Love*.

Ian's first love, and possibly still his greatest love, is live theater. "The recognition is a tangible force you can feel," he says. "I got to sing and dance, and when you come out for a curtain call and everyone is applauding you, your skin tingles. It was exhilarating and an experience I can still feel." For seven months he played Nils in *I Remember Mama* on Broadway, and then he played John in the national tour of *Peter Pan*. He had the experience of working with some truly great performers including Liv Ullmann, George Hearn, and George Rose.

But it was TV and, more specifically, the soaps where Ian Ziering really made his mark. When Luke Perry came to New York looking for a job on the soaps he met Ian, who was already established.

Ian's major daytime credit was two and a half years as Cameron Stewart on "Guiding Light." There were also recurring roles in various afternoon dramas including "Love of Life" and "The Doctors." There was a period when you couldn't turn on afternoon television without encountering Ian Ziering somewhere. He also had the lead in "Four Babies," an after-school special directed by Linda Lavin.

With all this going on, he still managed to make it through high school—his neighborhood high school, not a special school for young actors—and college. He graduated with a B.A. in dramatic arts from William Paterson College in Wayne, New Jersey. Did you expect this lifetime performer to have an M.B.A. from Harvard? The only career Ian ever considered, aside from acting, is marine biology. The subject fascinates him.

After Ian's part was written out of "Guiding Light," he spent a year out of work, and for a while he suffered from the actor's great fear: "I'll never work again." Then along came the "Class of Beverly Hills" audition. Within a week he heard he had the part of Steve Sanders, and he boarded a plane for California.

As a New York actor, Ian Ziering experienced a bit of culture shock after moving to California. A lot of New York actors have that feeling. A life that is almost entirely dependent on the automobile still bothers him. And he had to give up the large saltwater aquarium that he kept in his house in Morristown, New Jersey. But he's adjusting and thinking of taking up surfing.

Ian's character, Steve Sanders, is a Beverly Hills kid who seems to have everything—looks, personality, girls, money—and everything that money can buy, including the latest in designer clothes and a hot car. But Ian sees him as more complex. If his tough exterior is pierced, he reveals a vulnerable and possibly sensitive individual. "There's a certain dichotomy in my character," Ian explains. "He's on the edge of what is real and what is an illusion, which is somewhat typical of life in Beverly Hills."

Ian identifies with Steve in that they both have a great sense of humor, but Ian regards himself as more worldly, less gullible.

Though he's known on the set as a joker, Ian takes his part on this extremely popular and influential show very seriously. He speaks at high schools all over the country, and he feels that, "If I can help someone from turning in the wrong direction, then I feel good."

Ian is also an animal lover, though his pet is more conventional than Luke's pig. It's a two year old mixed-breed dog named Coty that Ian picked up from the pound. There is a park in Los Angeles where dogs are allowed to run free—a couple of hundred dogs running around on the grass. "What a sight," says Ian.

11 ☆ Gabrielle Carteris/ Andrea Zuckerman

☆
☆
☆
☆
☆
☆
☆

Gabrielle Carteris was told that she was too short to become a dancer. So she decided to become an actress. That sort of decision is typical of this dedicated—one might even say driven—young woman. She was also told that she wasn't pretty enough to succeed as an actress. She didn't let that stop her, either.

Gabrielle, like Brenda Walsh, has a twin brother. His name is James Ernest. They were born in Phoenix, Arizona, but they don't remember it at all. Their parents were divorced when the twins were about six months old, and her mother took them to San Francisco. Gabrielle says that she gets her drive from her mother, Marlene, who started her own children's clothing business and now runs a chain of stores.

Gabrielle did very well in school, which created a problem for her brother, who was no great shakes as a student. But after she started high school—after she was told that she would never be a professional dancer—Gabrielle's main focus was on acting. She also became an accomplished mime and, at the age of fourteen, spent a summer traveling through Europe with a troupe of professional mimes. She remembers that exciting summer as one of the high points of her young life.

A lot of young people with Gabrielle's ambition and talent would have headed directly for Hollywood or New York after graduation from high school. She thought about doing just that, but her mother was against it, and Gabrielle felt she wanted to know more about the world. "No one likes a stupid actor," she says. So she went to college.

Instead of attending a West Coast school, Gabrielle went to Sarah Lawrence College, a prestigious school in Bronxville, New York, just outside of New York City. Sarah Lawrence is strong in the arts, and Gabrielle also attended acting classes in the city. She then spent a year studying in England at the Royal Academy of Dramatic

Art and the London Academy of Music and Drama.

Being so close to New York, she started going to auditions and was able to pick up a bit of radio work and a few commercials. After graduation she got some important TV credits in the award-winning CBS after-school special "What If I'm Gay?" and in the ABC after-school specials "Seasonal Differences" and "Just Between Friends." She did soaps as well and had a small but recurring part in NBC's "Another World." There is one motion picture on her résumé —*Jacknife*, starring Robert De Niro and Ed Harris.

Live theater is still what most New York actors consider *real* acting, and Gabrielle was in several off-Broadway productions. Her biggest stage role was that of Cecile in the George Street Playhouse production of *Les Liaisons Dangereuses* in New Jersey.

Gabrielle Carteris seemed well on her way to becoming a New York actor. And like many New York actors she tended to look down her nose at Hollywood. She vowed that she would never even go out to the West Coast again unless she had a definite part. But the moment came when there was no New York work on the horizon for her, so she decided to go to Los Angeles during what is called "pilot season"—that's when auditions are being held for all the new TV shows.

Gabrielle made the rounds and almost immediately was offered a part. She would have taken it, too, if she hadn't heard about the auditions for "Class of Beverly Hills." She first tried out for the role of Brenda. As a twin she figured she had an advantage, and she even took a picture of her brother to the audition. She didn't get the part, but was offered the part of the brainy and intense Andrea Zuckerman.

The part seemed tailor-made for her, and Gabrielle admits that there are a lot of similarities between her and Andrea. "We are alike in spirit in terms of being righteous. I have a high sense of morality, but she's more conservative. I was a little more out-there."

She now lives in an apartment in the San Fernando Valley. She has a boyfriend named Charlie, a stockbroker who followed her to California when she moved from New York. She also has a parrot named Conya. And she's having the time of her life. "I'm very happy with what I'm doing right now," she said. "I am living out my dreams."

☆
☆
☆
☆
☆
☆
☆

12 ☆ Brian Austin Green/ David Silver

Brian Austin Green is one of only two cast members of "Beverly Hills, 90210" who started playing a high school student on the show while he really was old enough to be a high school student. (Tori Spelling is the other.) And he is the only member of the cast who uses his middle name. He may also be the most musically inclined, and he is certainly the best dancer. "A real rubber-band man," he has been called.

The character of David Silver started out as sort of a lovable geek. "I hope I'm not as geeky as David," says Brian. He isn't, but as far as the rest of the "90210" cast is concerned, Brian is certainly lovable. And his character, David, isn't as geeky as he once was, either. As the second semester at West Beverly High started, David had emerged as a sort of student leader, running the school radio station and the talent show. He may be captain of the football team next. Who knows?

In fact, the character of David just keeps on growing. "When the show was first written," Brian said in an interview given during the middle of the show's first season, "David wasn't a main character; he was just supposed to be in once in a while. Then when the second pilot was out, everyone really loved the character—they thought he was the comedy side of the whole thing. But the scripts had already been finished before the pilot was even shown, and they were all written with the intention of David being a little thing off to the side. The good news is, I had a meeting with the producer where we were talking about next season, and the characters are all going to develop a little more."

The lovable geek David Silver has developed a lot more. He's still funny, but he's a lot more self-assured, and he's more central to the action.

Though very young, Brian came to the series with a solid show-business background. His father, George Green, is a musician—a drummer who used to back up a lot of top acts during tours. He has now adopted the less hectic life of a studio musician; he plays on television shows. Brian inherited his father's musical talent and assumed that when he grew up he would go into the music business.

He was born and raised in the San Fernando Valley town of North Hollywood, in a house he says was built for a movie company. With his family and the show-business atmosphere of the entire region, it is hardly surprising that he went to a grammar school that specialized in the performing arts.

A graduate student in the film school at the University of Southern California asked eleven-year-old Brian to appear in a movie he was making as a school project. Brian did that one and a couple of others, and decided that acting was fun.

He got an agent, or rather his mother got him one, and within a few weeks he was picking up work. At first it was commercials and voice-overs. Then he landed a really solid part in the series "Knots Landing." He played Brian Cunningham, the son of Abby Ewing (Donna Mills). At first it seemed like a great opportunity for such a young actor, but eventually the ambitious and savvy Brian thought it limited him. He wasn't able to find other, more satisfying roles, and besides, as practically the only kid on the show, and on the set, he got lonely.

Even though he was tied to the grind of a series, Brian, a bundle of energy, did manage to find time for other roles. He made appearances in such shows as "Bay Watch," "Highway to Heaven," "Small Wonder," and "The New Leave It to Beaver." He also did the ABC miniseries "Baby M," "The Canterville Ghost," and "Good Morning, Miss Bliss." He earned several important screen credits in films like *An American Summer* and *Kickboxer II*. And just for a change, he played Tommy in a stage production of *Ah, Wilderness*.

Brian didn't do all of this work while holding down a role on a weekly series, though. After three years on "Knots Landing," Brian's character "moved away." He was written out of the show, and Brian was free to pursue his career elsewhere.

Brian's off-the-set life was very much that of a show-biz kid. During most of his time on "Knots Landing," he didn't go to a regular school but was tutored on the set. When he did go to school, it was to North Hollywood High, and his friends were mostly other show-business kids. He admits that he was not a great student.

As a result, when Brian tried out for a part on "Beverly Hills, 90210," he had a solid background as an actor, but not much of a background as a high school student. Still, he was the right age, and he could relate to the character. Like many other cast members, Brian thinks the show is more than just entertainment. "I think it is important because it is one of the few shows that really give out such positive messages."

When Brian was trying out for the part, his main competition was someone he already knew, another young actor named Douglas Emerson. Like Brian, Doug was already a seasoned professional. He had more than forty TV shows under his belt before the age of fifteen. There were lots of commercials and some movie credits on his résumé as well.

Brian and Doug had competed for parts before, and they had become friends. This time Brian won the role of David Silver, but Doug was given another role, that of Scott Scott, David's best friend.

Brian is still interested in music and thinks that someday he may still make music a major part of his career. He's also thinking about directing. In fact, there is practically no aspect of the entertainment business that Brian Austin Green is not thinking about.

13 ☆ Tori Spelling/ Donna Martin

Tori Spelling is the one cast member of "Beverly Hills, 90210" who is doubly fitted for the role: she is a teenager, and she was born in Beverly Hills. Not quite *in* Beverly Hills, but in the nearby and even more exclusive and expensive suburb of Bel Air. If her name sounds a bit familiar, it should. She is the daughter of Aaron Spelling, the producer of the show.

Tori and the show's publicists insist that Daddy didn't even know Tori had tried out and that he had nothing to do with her winning the part of Donna Martin, because she auditioned anonymously. That's a little hard to believe, since she was already a fairly well known actress who had appeared on numerous television shows. But then, Hollywood is a land of fantasy.

Just that sort of thinking has been a downside to Tori's life. "I'm not just another rich kid," she insists. She is not. She is a very, very rich kid. No matter what she does, no matter how good she is, there will always be the suspicion that she got her role because of her father's influence. In this case, it doesn't matter how she got the part. On-screen she *is* the popularity-crazed, often insensitive, and always funny Donna Martin. There may be some actresses who could have played the part as well as Tori. But nobody could have done it better.

If you think it's hard to imagine the life of the West Beverly High kids, with all their money, it's even harder to imagine the world in which Tori Spelling grew up. Aaron Spelling is Hollywood's most successful TV producer, and he does not hide that fact. He lives in what is reputedly the largest private home in the state of California. Tori doesn't even know how many rooms it has. It does have a private movie theater, a rose garden, a bowling alley, and an ice-skating rink. The family car was a limo, and Tori was embarrassed to go places in it, though she is not embarrassed or defensive about her family's wealth.

At school all her friends wanted to come

over to the house and meet her dad. Tori has learned to protect herself from being used.

A lot of the people Aaron Spelling worked with would drop over for a visit—people like Farrah Fawcett, Kate Jackson, and Linda Evans, some of the biggest stars in the business.

In spite of all of this, Tori insists that she had a normal childhood. Her parents did everything they could to help her turn out to be "just a regular kid." They seem to have succeeded. And like a lot of other regular and normal kids, Tori had dreams of becoming an actress. Her parents never pushed her in that direction, but if they had any reservations they never tried to discourage her, either. Still, it would be foolish to deny that she had a huge advantage.

At the age of six Tori made her television acting debut as a guest star on "Vega$." It was then that she was really bitten by the acting bug. "Even though I was pretty young, I really enjoyed the work. I knew that I wanted to continue acting because performing seemed natural to me."

She began to study acting and to pile up the screen credits. She appeared in such shows as "Hotel," "The Love Boat," "T. J. Hooker," and "Fantasy Island." Her first feature film was *Troop Beverly Hills*—she just can't seem to get away from the place—which starred Shelley Long.

When Aaron Spelling decided to produce "90210," he talked to Tori about casting, because she was young and she knew the sort of actors who could fill the roles. Tori suggested Jason Priestley and was enthusiastic about Shannen Doherty, because she had admired her work in the film *Heathers*.

Tori first tried out for the part of Kelly Taylor, but had to settle for the role of Donna, who was a recurring character but not a regular at first. However, the part of Donna has been beefed up as the show has progressed, and Tori is quite happy with it.

Like all the other cast members she thinks the show is important because "It sends the right message to teenagers."

TRIVIA

Amaze your friends with your knowledge of your favorite TV series:

☆ There is a real Beverly Hills High which served as the inspiration for the fictional West Beverly Hills High.

★ The real school has 1,900 students mostly from very wealthy families, just like on TV. The show, however, is not filmed at Beverly Hills High. The exteriors are shot at suburban Torrance High School in California's Orange County. It is a good school but distinctly less ritzy than the real Beverly Hills High School.

☆ When "Beverly Hills, 90210" was first aired there was a lot of criticism of the show at the real Beverly Hills High School. The school paper said it was a "joke" and according to *People* magazine some of the students resented being portrayed as rich, snobbish stereotypes. However, since "90210" has caught on, many opinions have changed. There is even a Club 90210 at Beverly Hills High.

★ When asked what clique she belonged to when she was in high school, Tori Spelling replied, "The most popular clique."

☆ Tori, who admits to being "surgically attached to the telephone" also carries a beeper.

★ Shannen Doherty drives a black BMW.

☆ Doug Emerson, who plays Scott Scott, was a veteran actor at the age of sixteen. He has a phenomenal memory and can recall every one of the sixty commercials and forty TV shows that he has been in.

★ Andrea Zuckerman, the brainiest of the "90210" gang is played by Gabrielle Carteris, the best educated of the cast members.

☆ Jason Priestley, who doesn't seem to take anything very seriously, originally told interviewers that he was from Borneo and that his father supported the family by fishing for squid. In reality he was born in Vancouver, Canada, and his family was in show business.

★ Though he tends to play it down in interviews, Luke Perry was miserable in his small town high school. "I was not a happy camper in Redneckville," he once confided.

☆ Jennie Garth has never played the character Peter Pan, but she has said, "I'm never going to be an adult."

★ Ian Ziering used to relax by watching the fish in his 55-gallon salt water aquarium. He says he found the activity "captivating and soothing."

☆ If he hadn't become an actor, Brian Austin Green says he would probably have been "a dirt farmer or a worm wrangler."

★ Sean Doherty, Shannen's brother, is married and his wife has a child, who Shannen adores. But she tries to avoid the title "Aunt Shannen."

☆ Jason Priestley goes out of his way to separate his private life from his "90210" character. He dresses differently, often does not shave and might not be recognized by his fans which is just fine with him, for he has said that the hardest thing about being a star is the loss of privacy. He also tends to resent interviewers who try to pierce this veil of privacy. When he was asked by Joan Rivers, "Are you single?" he didn't simply say yes. Rather his reply was, "Well, that's probably open to debate." Further probing brought forth this statement: "I have a girlfriend I've been dating for a long while. I'm not married. I try to keep my relationships private." When he was told that wasn't possible, he replied, "I can try."

★ In Hollywood circles the name of his girlfriend isn't all that secret. It's Robyn Lively, a young actress Jason met while filming *Teen Angel*. Like Jason, Robyn comes from a show biz background, and is well aware of the problems an acting career can create for any relationship.

☆ Luke Perry lives alone (except for the pig, of course) and does not admit to any long-term serious relationship at the moment. There was one when he was in New York, but Luke says, "It ended tragically— don't they all."

★ Shannen Doherty's favorite books are John Steinbeck's *East of Eden* and Ernest Hemmingway's *The Sun Also Rises*.

☆ Next to acting, Tori Spelling loves to write. She says that someday she may become a scriptwriter.

★ "I was a bit of a rebel," says Gabrielle Carteris of her own high school career. "I loved it when I could convince a teacher to teach outside or, instead of writing a paper, I'd organize a mime troupe to do something political."

☆ Aaron Spelling is a strange producer for a "message" show like "Beverly Hills, 90210." He is best known for such escapist fare as "The Love Boat" and "Fantasy Island." He has said that now, more than ever, TV viewers need shows like that. "I can't believe that we're not doing more television like (those shows). Look at how the audience responded to *Ghost*. There's a hunger for old-fashioned entertainment."

★ Spelling may have taken on "90210" because when the idea was offered to him, it was the first time in many years that he didn't have a single series. He was once TV's most prolific producer. He was hurt by headlines in the entertainment press which said things like "Spelling Dynasty Dead." He hasn't seen any headlines like that recently.

☆ Spelling says that "90210" has changed since it premiered. "Then it was a high school show; now it's about the joys and traumas of being a teen."

★ One of the few (very few) TV critics to recognize the quality of "90210" early on was John Voorhees of the *Seattle Times*. His quote, "Watch it for a couple of weeks and you may get hooked as I am," appeared in much of the early promotional literature for the show. The show didn't have many other good quotes from the critics. Voorhees deserves the TV critics' "crystal ball award" if there is one.

☆ "I was a social butterfly in high school," admits Jennie Garth.

★ Jason Priestley may be a little dissatisfied with Brandon Walsh's good guy image. *"Brandon,"* he says. "What's there to *say* about Brandon." He has hinted that Brandon will be getting into a little more trouble in the future, that he will be shedding some of that straight-arrow image. But if you ask him what kind of trouble, his lips are sealed. Future plans for the show are closely guarded secrets, and all plans are subject to change.

☆ Cast members have been advised to play down their real life love stories, so as not to interfere with the image of the characters they play. They want all the fans out there to think that there is still hope for *them*. They don't want to destroy the fantasy.

★ "I try not to date actors," says Shannen Doherty.

☆ Luke Perry says that "90210" is "the best show on television, except for 'Jeopardy'!"

★ Series creator Darren Star has a sister named Bonnie. Their mother says she is struck by the resemblance between Jason Priestley and Shannen Doherty, and Darren and his sister. "I sometimes think he's gotten some of the words right out of his sister's mouth. She (Shannen) even resembles Bonnie. And the boy has so many of Darren's personality traits. When I watch the show I miss my kids like crazy."

☆ Darren Star is thoroughly enjoying his wildly unexpected "Beverly Hills, 90210" success, and has recently purchased a Porsche. If things keep going the way they appear to be, there may even be a Rolls-Royce in his future.

★ James Eckhouse, who plays understanding father James Walsh, had originally intended to be a scientist. He studied physics and biology at MIT, in Cambridge, Massachusetts, one of the nation's top science schools, before turning to acting.

☆ "When you have a lot of hype around a show, it puts a lot of pressure on," Eckhouse has told interviewers. "I just hope this show will be allowed to have its own life."

★ Carol Potter (Cindy Walsh) is best known for her work on the Broadway stage, although she had appeared with star Mike Connors in the ABC television series "Today's FBI." Her first major acting break-through came when she played Judith Hastings in the long-running Broadway show *Gemini.*

☆Initially the "90210" producers were very unhappy with the 9 P.M. time slot that Fox had put them in. "This one is death," Darren Star told the *Washington Post* in December of 1990. "This would be a great eight o'clock show. After nine o'clock kids have to go to bed." As it turned out they weren't going to bed, they stayed up watching the show and the nine o'clock time has remained. No one is complaining anymore.

★The themes of many of the "90210" shows will coincide with the time the episodes air. There will be a Christmas show, a back to school show, etc. Advertisers love that.

☆ Jason Priestley says that he never gets nervous working, but "I get nervous being myself."

★ Shannen Doherty, who has been able to face down television producers (some of the scariest people on earth) says that she is terrified of horror films.

☆ One of the questions Shannen is most frequently asked is what it's like to kiss Luke Perry. The actress's response, "You don't understand. You have about forty people watching you."

★ Information on the various "90210" stars is often filled with contradictions. One of the biggest concerns Shannen Doherty's eating habits. Some accounts say that she loves junk food, burgers and fries, and eats twenty-four-hours a day without gaining weight. According to other sources, she carefully watches her diet, "eats healthy," limits her consumption of red meat, and exercises constantly in her free time to keep her weight in check. You may take your pick as to which version of the Shannen Doherty diet and health plan you wish to believe.

☆ Gabrielle Carteris was inspired to go into mime by her friendship with a deaf girl in high school.

★ Director Charles Braverman refuses to admit that "90210" is a difficult show to work on. "This is not a high-pressure show," he insists.

☆ Perhaps the most famous line from "90210" came early on when Kelly told newcomer Brenda, "You make one false move and you're history."

★ To give you an idea of how a show can change, some of the early publicity shots of the stars of "90210" don't contain Luke Perry. Dylan was not originally slated to be a major character. In wartime there is a phrase "battlefield promotion." Luke has certainly earned one, on the TV battlefield.

☆ Luke Perry's pet pig is named after rock-and-roll pioneer Jerry Lee Lewis. It was given to him as a birthday present, but he won't say who gave it to him. Jerry Lee Lewis, as you might guess, is one of Luke's favorite performers.

★ When living in New York, Luke developed a passion for bagels. One of his big complaints about living in Los Angeles is, "I have to drive three miles out here, just to get bagels and whitefish." What, no lox, Luke?

☆ "I just live for fan mail," says Tori Spelling.

★ Fighting against drugs has been one of Brian Austin Green's major offscreen activities. "For the past two years I've been on a celebrity bike team. It's me, Jeremy Miller, Jenny Lewis, Andre Gower, David Faustino, and some others, and what we've done is tour around the country and talk to kids about drugs. What we're trying to do is push the idea that instead of getting high on drugs, you can get 'high' off things you enjoy, like sports—or anything you really like, including biking."

☆ Jason Priestley, who admits that he was no angel in high school, (though he played one on TV) recalls one incident that really shocked him. At a wild drinking party in eleventh grade a girl he knew locked herself in the bathroom and tried to slit her wrists with a razor blade. Jason is convinced that alcohol contributed to her depression and attempted suicide.

★ Shannen is a big Madonna fan, not so much for the singer's music but for her astounding ability to market herself and her shrewd business sense. Madonna is now one of the highest-paid performers in America.

☆ Jason has a weird taste in entertainment. His favorite TV show was the very weird (and now canceled) "Twin Peaks." His favorite film is the strange and scary *A Clockwork Orange*, directed by Stanley Kubrick.

★ Gabrielle Carteris's last name is Greek (not French as everyone seems to think). Her favorite book is the feminist novel *The Handmaid's Tale* by Margaret Atwood.

About the Author

Daniel Cohen is the author of over a hundred books for both young readers and adults, and he is a former managing editor of *Science Digest* magazine. His titles include *The Greatest Monsters in the World, Real Ghosts, The Restless Dead: Ghostly Tales from Around the World, The Monsters of Star Trek, Going for the Gold: Medal Hopefuls for Winter '92* (co-authored with Susan Cohen), and *Beverly Hills, 90210: Meet the Stars of Today's Hottest TV Series,* all of which are available in Archway Paperback editions. His Minstrel titles include *Ghostly Terrors, The World's Most Famous Ghosts,* and *Phone Call from a Ghost.*

Mr. Cohen was born in Chicago and has a degree in journalism from the University of Illinois. He has lectured at colleges and universities throughout the country. Mr. Cohen lives with his wife in New York.